ALASKAN RESCUE

ALASKAN RESCUE

TIMOTHY PETERS

ABUNDANT HARVEST
PUBLISHING

Formatting: Erik V. Sahakian
Cover Design/Layout/Photo: Andrew Enos
Inside Artwork: Brittney Peters

All Scripture is taken from the New King James
Version of the Bible. Copyright © 1979, 1980, 1982 by
Thomas Nelson, Inc. Used by permission. All rights
reserved.

Library of Congress Control Number: 2019938191

ISBN 978-1-7327173-6-7
Second Printing: September 2019

FOR INFORMATION CONTACT:

Abundant Harvest Publishing
35145 Oak Glen Rd
Yucaipa, CA 92399
www.abundantharvestpublishing.com

Printed in the United States of America

TABLE OF CONTENTS

For my son, Jeremiah, his wife, Brittney, and their children, Benaiah, Guinevere, and Amos.

Chapter 1

"Dad! Bear! Bear! Dad!" Fifteen-year old Josh Powers shouted at the top of his lungs. A flash of furry brown hair and a fearless growl had caught his attention.

His father, Doug Powers, a missionary pilot, stood on top of a large boulder at the edge of a cliff, gazing at Alaska's snowcapped mountains and crystal clear rivers. When he heard his son's desperate warning, he turned just in time to see a giant brown bear charging toward him. "Run! Joshua, run!" he shouted. Doug Powers ran, but in his haste tripped on the loose rocks and fell over the edge.

"Dad!" Josh ran toward the edge of the cliff, but suddenly put on the brakes when he found himself face to face with the bear—less than 20 feet away. He tried to remember everything the survival books had taught him, but his brain drew a blank. He took a few deep breaths. His hands shook, though everything else on his body seemed to freeze up. *Lord, please scare this bear off?*

The bear stood on her hind legs. She was a giant, about twice his size with paws as big as a catcher's glove. His instinct was to run, but he was sure she would outrun him. *This is what David must have felt like when he faced Goliath*, he thought. Josh reached down and grabbed a long, thick stick, held it over his head and not knowing if this was his last moment on earth yelled "Aaaah," waving the stick wildly through the air. The bear, a little startled, stood her ground.

As they stared each other down (Josh mainly out of fear), two bear cubs came tumbling out of the bush. They playfully clawed at each other, brawling through the bushes before running in another direction, away from Josh. When the cubs disappeared under a fallen tree trunk, the mother bear lowered down on all fours.

"Okay," Josh said as he looked for his escape. "Just a momma bear protecting her cubs. I can respect that."

Then unexpectedly, the bear took three steps toward him, raised her paw, swiped it through the air, and roared. It was Josh's turn to stand his ground and, out of character, roared back. Mother bear, more interested with her cubs' whereabouts, had lost interest in her human adversary as she turned and walked off through the woods.

Josh blew out a big sigh of relief. "Yeah, you better run."

The young pilot then hurried to the boulder where he last saw his father. "Dad, are you okay? Can you hear me?" He scrambled closer to the edge. No sign of his dad. "Dad, where are you!" Climbing down a few feet, clutching the jutting rocks and roots, he called out again. "Dad, where are you?" This time he heard a muffled voice coming from somewhere below. Finally, about fifteen feet below, he found his dad lying on a wide, smooth ledge.

"I wouldn't recommend it, Son, but this was one way to ditch a charging bear." His dad managed a half smile.

"Diving over a cliff?" Josh shook his head. "Brilliant! Are you all right?"

"I think I broke my leg and my pack frame hit my ribs. They're very sore. I think they're broken, too."

"You fell a long way. Lie still, as still as you can. I'm coming down to you." Josh secured a rope around a tree and climbed down. "Let's see if I can get you up. Let's tie this rope around you."

"Stop, stop!" Doug Powers shouted when Josh tried to help him up. "That's not going to work."

"Sorry. Didn't mean to hurt you."

Doug Powers moaned with every twist and turn. His voice was raspy. "You'll have to find something to truss up my ribs and splint my leg."

Josh nodded. Taking his knife, he carefully cut all the straps off his dad's pack frame, and pulled it clear from under him. Then looked through the backpack for something to use and found a flannel shirt. "Will this work?"

"That should work fine. You don't want to make it so tight that it displaces my ribs. You only want to make it tight enough to hold them in place, and then around my arm so it won't move. It's going to hurt, but it has to be done."

Josh spread out the arms of the shirt. Placing the back over the broken ribs, he pulled the sleeves around his father's chest, tying the first knot in the sleeves.

Doug Powers gasped. "Okay, make it a little tighter. Not much, just a little."

Josh shook his head, took hold of the sleeves, and gently pulled them together.

"Good, Joshua." Doug Powers clenched his teeth as Josh tied off the shirt with a second knot. "Good. Now find something to make a sling."

"The belly strap off the backpack should do." Josh put the pad around his dad's neck. He worked fast, sighed a couple of times as he took one end of the strap, putting it under the red flannel shirt before buckling it. Slowly, he raised his father's hand, moving it toward the sling and
slipping it gently into the opening.

"That's better. At least that's as good as it will get for now."

"I'll find something to splint your leg." Josh straightened up. "I'll be back in a minute."

"I'll wait right here for you."

Josh chuckled as he looked at his father. "That's a bad joke, Dad." *Just like you to crack a few bad jokes to keep me from worrying.* He climbed up the side of the cliff and got back on the trail searching the ground for a flat piece of wood; about three feet long would do it. Lucky for him he found it within minutes of his search and returned to his father.

"Sorry Joshua, you're going to need another splint just like that, one for each side of my leg."

Josh ruffled his brown hair. "All right. I'll be right back." It took longer this time but he came back with yet another piece of flat wood about one foot longer. With his Swiss Army knife Josh started the long, slow process of cutting the wood to the same length.

"Too bad we don't have the time to soak up this magnificent view." As far as they could see there were tall trees. He breathed in the different smells of the plants and enjoyed the squeals and chirps of the birds before resuming the task at hand. "This is the most beautiful place I have ever seen."

"I think you're right, Son. There's never a better time or place to thank our heavenly Father for everything." Doug Powers bowed his head. "Thank You, God, for sparing my life. Guide Joshua over the next few days and give him strength. In Jesus' name, amen."

"Amen," Josh mumbled under his breath. He really needed God to tell him how to get his dad back up the cliff. *I'll thank Him later*, he thought. Carrying him was out of the question. It was too steep. Dragging him was not an option. It would probably injure him even more. And with civilization far away, and no help in sight, Josh would have to come up with a rescue plan on his own.

"Dad, looks like we're stuck for the night." Josh rubbed his hands together. "We're kind of exposed out here and it's getting dark, we'll have to get you back on the trail tomorrow."

"That's fine, Son." Doug Powers closed his eyes. "Whatever you think is best."

The next few days, Josh knew, would depend on his skills. Plans brewed in his mind. "I hope this doesn't hurt you too much." He finally sawed through the piece of wood.

Kneeling by his father's broken leg, he placed a board on each side. One of the straps he had cut off the pack frame was tied around the two pieces of wood at the thigh. Doug Powers gritted his teeth and writhed in pain when his son pulled the wood together at his ankle. But Josh continued as he took the last strap, tying it securely around the wood.

"I have to leave you one more time, Dad. We need another strap off my backpack."

His father nodded, sucking air through his clinched teeth.

As Josh neared the top of the trail it began to rain. "Great," he muttered. Quickly he cut the two shoulder straps of his backpack and headed back.

"Take a deep breath, Dad," he said as he tied one strap tight around the leg right under the knee. The other strap he used to tie the break. His dad shivered. "Here you go." Josh pulled out the tent and sleeping bag from his dad's pack. He unrolled the sleeping bag, carefully slid it under his dad, and the tent provided shelter.

"You better take a couple of painkillers," Josh said. He placed the pills in his father's open mouth, and gave him a drink of cool water from his canteen. "I'll gather all the firewood we need for tonight. Try to get some sleep."

Two hours had passed since their encounter with the bear and Josh was starving. The granola bar didn't do it for him. He ate another bar and saved the last two for his dad.

It would take him several trips to gather the firewood. *At least the bears won't get us here,* Josh thought. He remembered talking to a Forest Ranger before they left on this backpacking trip. The ranger had told them to make sure they didn't have food in their tent at night. He also said the island had more bears than people. Josh shuddered.

He picked up an armload of kindling wood and crawled down to the ledge. With small rocks he made a u-shape and stacked the kindling inside. Then he reached into his pocket and pulled out the dried Sitka spruce needles to start his fire.

As he breathed in the cold, fresh air he placed the needles under the wood and struck the match he had taken from his waterproof container. The needles caught fire and ignited the wood. Its flames were a welcomed companion. Josh rubbed his hands together over the friendly fire. Soon he felt warm all over.

"You were gone a long time. Everything okay?" Doug Powers opened his eyes.

"Yeah, I had to gather a big pile of wood for our fire tonight. Here are two granola bars. You better eat them."

"Have you seen another bear?"

"No, but I've been watching." Josh took some of the bigger logs and laid them on the hot, glowing coals. It took a while for them to catch but soon the fire crackled and snapped in the night air. "This will help you get through the long night, Dad. I'm going to get my backpack now, then I'll be down here the rest of the night."

Doug Powers nodded as he chewed the last of his granola bars.

But as Josh wearily climbed back up, he encountered another bear. "Oh, man, just what I need." It was very interested in his backpack. Josh ducked behind the boulder. Even though this bear wasn't as big as the other one, he wasn't about to challenge it.

His heart raced as he crawled behind the highest point of the boulder. Somehow he had to keep the bear from shredding his backpack and sleeping bag as it sniffed the bag. Without another thought, which might have changed his mind, Josh jumped onto the highest part of the boulder and with his hands waving over his head shouted, "Bear! Get!" Then he jumped back down out of sight. Josh peeked around the edge of the boulder. It seemed he had alarmed it.

"Here goes nothing." He jumped in full view of the bear. "Bear! Get! Get out of here! The bear stood frozen, staring at him. "Oh boy. God, make this creature go away!" To Josh's relief, the bear's attention turned to the wind blowing through the thickets behind it. Josh watched it lumber away, snapping twigs with each step. When it was out of sight he raced toward his pack, slid into his pack feet first, just like he used to do when sliding into second base, scooped it up, hauled back to the boulder, and almost flew down the side of the cliff toward his father where he finally felt safe again—out of breath, but safe. "There was an ... another bear ... bear up there."

"Another bear? I heard you yelling, but couldn't make out what you said. It wasn't the same bear, was it? That one was a hairy rug with an attitude."

Josh chuckled as he threw more wood on the fire. The weather wasn't getting any better. It got darker and the rain increased. Josh sat by the fire that burned safely beneath a dense canopy of leafy branches overhanging from the side of the cliff. "Dad," he whispered. "Do you think that hell lasts forever?"

It was a question that came out of left field, but that's where Josh's thoughts wandered.

"Very likely, I'm afraid. This world is broken and I think God's judgement is real and terrible. The Bible talks about eternal fire and darkness, but I don't know how that happens. That's why we chose to be missionaries." Doug Powers breathed into his free hand. "We want to tell people how to have hope in Jesus and totally avoid the eternal fire thing."

"I like sharing the love of God, not so much the damnation thing, though." Josh believed it was his responsibility as a Christian to talk about God's love with others. But he was always afraid, though he didn't know of what. "Wasn't it Paul who said he wasn't ashamed of the gospel of Christ?"

His father didn't answer as he had fallen asleep. Josh pulled his sleeping bag out of its sack and huddled under the tent that covered his dad. He closed his eyes but his mind continued to question. *Is that what's wrong with me? Am I ashamed?* Josh scooted beside his dad and drifted to sleep.

Chapter 2

Throughout the night Josh tossed more wood onto the flames to keep the fire burning. It didn't help much. He shivered from head to toe. Blowing warmth into his cupped hands did little to relieve his misery as the night grew colder. He gave up trying to sleep and decided to figure out how to get his dad off the ledge.

Dawn came, and Josh's eyes were wide open as he lay next to the fire. He noticed a tree branch hanging high over the ledge. *That might come in handy,* he thought. *Glad I packed that rope.*

He remembered his father's words before leaving on their journey. "Tie this climbing rope onto your backpack. We're going to need it. And these carabiners and belaying devise too."

He had questioned his dad on why they were taking so much stuff. "The 100 feet of bright blue climbing rope seems a bit much." They hadn't used the rope at all on their Alaskan adventure until now.

Josh eyed the tree branch, which slanted downward but still out of his reach. Its bark was peeled like someone had needed it before. He stood right underneath it, his forehead furrowed. *Maybe I could tie the belaying device onto the branch by the small hole and use the bigger hole for the pulley. But how am I going to get it up there?*

He dug inside his pack for the canvas bag with the four carabiners and the belaying device. Cutting the last strap off his backpack, he untied the rope from the frame and climbed the rock toward the tree. With the branch about an arm's length from his fingertips, Josh would have to jump and pull himself up. *Could be tricky, but I can do it.*

Josh worked through the early hours of the morning and set his plan in motion. First he uncoiled the rope and put one end of it through the larger hole of the belaying device. Then he pulled about half the rope through. He took one end and tied it to the trunk of the tree and placed the strap through the smaller hole tying it to his wrist so he wouldn't drop it over the edge. When he was ready to go, he examined the tree and admired his work.

"Well, here goes!" He crouched, then leapt straight up stretching his body, his arms, and his fingers as he reached for that elusive branch. He missed. Thump! Down onto the rock below he fell with a thwack that echoed through his chest. Stubbornly, he dusted himself off and tried again.

"Aaaah, come on!" he yelled as both hands latched onto the branch.

Josh pulled himself up onto the hefty branch into a sitting position facing the trunk of the tree. Then with surprising agility he turned around and sat with his legs dangling below the branch and his back against the trunk. He took a moment to stretch out the muscles in his arms and the crick in his neck. Gingerly he untied the strap holding the belaying device and the rope on his wrist, and tied the strap around the tree branch.

"That should do it."

When Josh climbed down, however, he realized the end of the rope had landed nowhere near his father. He sighed. This meant he would have to move the pulley out farther on the branch or risk dragging his father across the rocks. Not an easy task as the farther out the strap and rope got, the more the branch sagged. It wasn't strong enough. He aborted the plan.

Dejected, Josh grabbed the branch and swung his legs down, but with his mind on other things, his hands slipped off and once again he fell with a loud thud to the ground below. And if that wasn't bad enough, he tripped on the uneven rocks. His legs flailed about as he fell, skinning the backs of both legs. He moaned.

"Don't think about the pain," he told himself. "Dad still needs to be brought up from that ledge." He rolled over and lifted his tired and aching body off the unforgiving ground.

Josh wouldn't allow himself a spare minute. *Plan B it is.* "I have got to find a sturdy log." He walked around the now infamous boulder and spotted the perfect place where he thought he could lift his father clear: the part of the cliff that came straight up about fifteen feet. It seemed he could lift his father from there, out of the sling, without hurting him too badly.

"God always provides." He hummed while crawling back to his dad. "Dad, wake up."

"There you are, Son! I was a little worried."

"Yeah, yeah, sorry about that. But Dad, I figured out a way to get you out of here." Josh retrieved a pan from his dad's backpack and prepared for breakfast. "It's going to take some time to get set up though. And I'll have to walk you over there about twenty feet."

"Is there a way up to the trail there?"

"No, I'll have to rig something." Josh filled the pan with powdered eggs and a bit of water. "Don't worry, it'll work."

Eggs and freeze-dried bacon bits sizzled in the pan making both father and son hungry. Doug Powers took his breakfast and bowed his head. "We are thankful for this meal You have provided. Give Joshua wisdom and strength today to do the task ahead. In Jesus' name, amen."

Josh rekindled the fire. "That should take some of the chill out of us."

Warm eggs and crunchy bacon satisfied their hunger. Breakfast had never tasted so good as they gazed at the beautiful scenery, watching the sunlight creep up the rocks and trees across the valley from their outcropping.

Josh took out some painkillers. "Dad, I want you to take these so you'll be ready for the lift."

"The lift?"

"Yeah." Josh took a deep breath. "It's the only way to get you out. This won't be easy and it will take a while for me to get ready. I don't have time to tell you the details but you better take those pills."

After breakfast Josh began his search for a sturdy log. "About five or six inches in diameter, ten or twelve feet long." He mumbled to himself. He stayed away from the thick brush where he had encountered the bear. But his search wasn't going well. Most of the logs he found were too long, too heavy, or rotten, or still attached to the stump. This was going to be harder than he thought.

Blowing out a few deep breaths, he decided to hike back to "The Rock," as he had named it, and go up from there so he could pull a log downhill. It wouldn't matter how big the log was if he could drag it downhill. At least that's what he told himself.

Rain hindered his search as he buttoned up his blue flannel shirt. Still, he hiked passed a wall of rocks, into a meadow, before choosing to enter the forest off-trail. He stopped and checked each fallen tree. The search proved futile. Discouraged, hands on his waist and shaking his head, he thought about changing plans again. *Maybe I should get a stack of firewood for Dad, leave him with enough food, and go get help. He would be safe on the ledge.* Josh sat down on a rock, planted his forehead on his knees and flung his arms over his head. "God, You know my dad needs help. What I planned doesn't seem to be working. Perhaps you have a better plan. Please give me Your plan. Let me know what to do. In Jesus' name, amen."

He had made up his mind to go for help when something caught his eye just before he got to the meadow—a good-sized thick branch, broken off and leaning against the trunk of a tree. The rain had soaked the plants growing around it, drenching his clothes even more. He walked timidly toward the branch, looking in both directions for any angry territorial bear.

The branch was about five inches in diameter and tapered down to four inches on one end. He frowned, not sure if it would hold his father's weight? It was also older than he expected. When he pushed it away from the tree its bark flew everywhere. He would have to put it to the test first.

Josh picked up the sappy end of the log and dragged it. Though it was easier than carrying it on his shoulder, the log seemed to get heavier and sticky sap continued to ooze into his hands. When the log began to bounce across the tops of the underbrush, and with another two miles to go, Josh decided to take a breather. He could only afford a short one and soon he was dragging his log to "The Rock."

Josh went to work on the next stage of his plan. He placed the thicker end of the log under the rock outcropping and the other end, with a short branch still attached, hung out over the shelf. Two more rocks were needed to lean up against the log so it wouldn't roll. He wiped the sweat off his face with his bandana right after he put the first rock in place. "I didn't know you could sweat here."

The second rock, though a little smaller still took him 45 minutes to secure. Then his next steps had to go in perfect order: untie the rope from the tree; get the strap with the belaying device onto the end of the log; slide the log out, tie the strap to it, and put the log back in place; roll both support rocks away; lift the log out from under the crevice; tie the strap and belaying device onto the log above its branch; take the 100-foot rope and feed one end through the lower hole in the device and pull it to the middle; move the log back down to the hole under the rock outcropping and set the log in place; secure; roll the other two rocks back into place; take the tangle of rope and throw both ends down to the ledge.

At the end of the day, when he could finally stand up straight to stretch his back, Josh looked out over the lush, green valley. Clouds hung low and slowly drifted over and around the top of their ledge.

It's going to be another cold night. I better get more wood.

Chapter 3

The young pilot tried to warm himself by the fire. He had spent yet another night tending to it. Even so, he shivered for most of the time. Daylight was not much better as a cloud covered them like a furry blanket; a heavy mist soaked just about everything.

Josh rummaged through both packs looking for food. Freeze-dried spaghetti was the only thing left on the menu. They were supposed to get back to the airplane the night before and had planned on a big crab dinner in Hoonah.

"It's not crab." Josh held up the package of spaghetti.

"Looks great to me. We'll have to eat off the land for the next few days. You know this island is a smorgasbord."

"Glad to see you're still positive, given your predicament." Josh glanced toward his father while he cooked the freeze-dried spaghetti. "You're going to have to tell me how to tie a knot that won't slip. All I can tie are slipknots."

"I can do that. Why don't you bring me the rope? I'll tie a bosun's chair into the end of it."

Josh picked up the end of the rope and drug it around to his dad.

"Sit down here and watch how to do this." Doug Powers explained every step.

Josh would have to practice before he could get it perfect. It was a little confusing at times to follow the directions as Doug Powers could only use his one good hand and his teeth.

"How did you learn to do that?"

"When I was in the Navy about a hundred years ago. I've used that knot a lot since then."

"A hundred years ago huh?" Josh picked up the rope and after a few more practices tossed it back to his father. "Before we do anything else, I think it's time for a spaghetti breakfast. Let's eat."

"Even out here," Doug Powers said, "let's not forget to pray." He took one slow cleansing breath. "God, we thank You for this beautiful day and we thank You for the food You have supplied for us. Thank You for your protection in this wild land. Please guide our steps. Teach us what we need to learn today. In Jesus' name, amen."

"What do you think God wants us to learn today?" Josh asked.

"I guess we'll find out. Relying totally on Him would be my guess, and for strength and courage. But why don't you ask Him?"

Josh stared into the fire. "Lord, what do You want *me* to learn today?" He shrugged his shoulders.

After breakfast Josh gathered up all their belongings and hauled them up to the top of the rocks. His dad's sleeping bag which would be used to cushion the rope was left at the base of the cliff. "Well, Dad. It's time."

"Let's get 'er done!"

"Where does it hurt? Josh put his hand on Doug Powers' shoulder.

"Take my good arm in one hand and put your other hand right under my arm pit. I'll help you as much as I can. Once I get up on one leg, I should be fine." But a look of pain shot across his face as soon as Josh picked him up.

"Let's try it again," Josh said.

"No ... no," Doug Powers gritted his teeth, "just keep going." Once on his good leg he paused to steady himself.

"You ready?"

"Yeah! I'm good."

"We have to get around this corner about twenty feet away."

"Okay. Come to my left side. I'll use you like a crutch."

Josh raised his dad's left arm and slipped under it. But they got their signals crossed. As Josh stepped forward his dad stepped back causing them both to stumble, but Josh managed to keep them from falling.

"Wow! That was close! Let's try it again. Count the cadence."

"Okay Dad, let's both start with the left side." The step went off without a problem. It took Josh fifteen minutes, however, to help his dad go around the corner. There was no way Doug Powers could walk the five miles to where they were supposed to meet the floatplane.

I hope someone is looking for us, Josh thought.

Finally, with his father safely sitting beneath the log, Josh picked up the rope and slipped it over his dad's feet. "We have to put the sleeping bag under you so the rope doesn't cut your backside. You're going to sit in the bosun's chair, then I'll go up to the top to pull you up."

His dad nodded, "Did you think this up?"

"Pretty smart, huh?" Josh put the sleeping bag between his dad and the rope. Then he picked up the other end of it, coiled it up, and threw it to the top of the boulder.

Once he got to the top he tied his dad on, in case he couldn't hold onto the rope with one hand. When Josh came back down he found a piece of parachute cord in the bottom of his dad's backpack.

"I'm going to tie you onto the rope so you won't fall off." He put the cord around his dad, snugging it tight. "That should do it."

With his dad secured Josh made his way back up the rock. Walking to the edge, he dropped the coil down. But as he pulled on the rope Josh suddenly slipped and fell.

"You okay, Son?"

"Yeah, I'm fine."

"Wrap the rope around a tree; it will work like a pulley."

Across the trail Josh found a dead tree without its bark. He wrapped the rope around it and tied the end around his waist. "Are you ready?"

"Yes! Go ahead! Pull!"

Josh pulled with all the strength he had.

"That's it, Son! I'm a foot off the ground. Keep pulling!"

Doug Powers slowly ascended. Josh could see the top of his head.

"Just a few more pulls, Joshua!"

He grunted and groaned and with one more yell, Josh made his final pull.

"That's it! You did it! Now tie the rope off."

After tying the rope around the tree a few times he threw the end over the top and tied it off. Doug Powers was up, out of danger. Now all he had to do was get him off the rope and onto solid ground.

"Okay, Dad. I'm moving the log now." Josh reached out and pulled on the log. It slid over toward the edge just like it was meant to do, but then it stopped. "Looks like it hit part of the rock that's sticking up."

"Can you lift the log over?"

"I tried. It won't budge."

"Get a lever, Son."

Josh picked up a stick, placed it under the log and made another rock a fulcrum. "There may be a little bump when the log goes over the rock."

"Let 'er fly!"

Pressing down on the stick lifted the log, which then went up and over the rock with ease, but when it landed, it began to split. Josh jumped over it and pulled it toward him. It crackled and snapped.

"No!" Josh reached for his dad. Somehow he got a hold of him and grabbed him with a firm hand. He pulled and pulled, finally dragging his dad over the ledge. And just in time, too. The log shattered in to pieces, but Dough Powers was safe. "That was close!"

"You think? Maybe you should look for help, Joshua."

"No, not yet." Josh sat down to catch his breath. "I don't want to leave you alone. Besides, it's downhill from here except for one part where we have to go over the pass. We'll manage." He gathered the things they would need for the journey, while his dad rested.

He untied the rope from the tree and wound it into a neat coil, then freed the belaying device from the broken log.

"We have to decide what we need to take with us." Josh laid everything useful neatly on the ground. "We can't carry the packs because I cut the straps off. And we'll have to find something to eat. Maybe some sort of edible plant."

He hated to leave their packs out here in the wilderness, but he couldn't carry them and help his dad.

"We'll need the rope," Josh whispered.

Doug Powers laughed. "See, we did need the rope!"

"Yeah, you were right ... again." Josh picked up the rope, carabiner, and the belaying device and started another pile. "We may need the tent and sleeping bags as well."

At last, before setting out on the journey Josh sat down to enjoy his surroundings. The forest was thick, covered with ferns and giant skunk cabbage. Purple Fireweed grew in beautiful clusters. The star-shaped Salmonberry completed the ground cover and a sweet fragrance filled the air.

Josh opened the small Bible he had in his pocket to First Samuel and read the story of the Philistines putting the Ark of the Covenant on a cart drawn by two milk cows and sending it back to the children of Israel.

"That's what I need! A cart."

But there was no way he could make a cart because he didn't have a wheel. He tried to picture a cart without wheels. "A travois!" He remembered this from an old black and white movie they watched once when they came home from the mission field—Indians pulling all their belongings behind a horse on two sticks.

I could do that! Josh thought. *I'll need two long, but strong branches. That's all. I'll make a bed, and put my dad on it and pull him down the hill.* "Thank You Lord. You really do come through."

Chapter 4

Josh picked up three thick green branches, each about fifteen feet long, and drug them down the trail. "Dad, remember that old western movie, "Survivor at Alabama Hills" that Grandma used to have?" Before Doug Powers could answer Josh continued. "The Indians moved their whole village using a travois. That's what I'll make to get you out of here."

"Sounds like a good idea, Joshua. Do you think you can pull it off, since we're short on horses?"

Josh rolled his eyes. "Funny." He continued shaving the bark off the branches with his father's hunting knife. The bark came off in long strips. *I can do this,* he thought.

Once in a while doubt crept in. Would he really be able to drag the travois and a full-grown man down the hill? His dad wasn't very big, but neither was he. He closed his eyes for a second and prayed. "God please help me with this. Give me the strength I need. Amen!"

Josh heard his father's soft groans and shallow breaths. Only two Tylenol tablets remained. Those he saved in case the pain worsened. He had to work fast. The thought of going for help stayed in the back of his mind.

Josh worked the bark until it was smooth creating three sturdy poles. He cut about two feet off each pole to make them a manageable length. Two poles he would use for the sides of the travois, and the other pole he cut in half. He had everything he needed except a way to fasten them together.

"Dad, how am I going to hold this together? I don't have any nails. I need some vines or something."

"Use the remaining parachute cords in the bottom of my backpack."

Josh rummaged through the backpack and pulled out a large bundle of cord. "You think this stuff is strong enough?"

"If you wrap it around several times. People stake their lives on it every day."

Josh nodded as he lay the poles out on the ground—the two long poles parallel, then the two shorter poles across.

"The poles are too far apart, Joshua. We could tie a horse between those."

"I know, Dad. I'm just trying to make it comfortable for you."

Josh moved the two poles closer together. Hopefully he would have enough room at the ends to pull and still be narrow enough to fit most of the trails. "Just making sure you don't fall off." Josh winked.

Doug Powers acknowledged his son with a nod. Then using the saw blade on his Swiss Army knife, Josh whittled away the end of each crosspiece. "Done," he said. "Now to tie one end of the cord around the pole and wrap it over the two poles where they cross."

He pulled each wrap of the cord as tight as he could and repeated this process the other way across the joint to make an "X." He did this several times in each direction and then tied it off. "There." He dusted off his hands. "That should strengthen the joint."

Tying off the second joint, he moved the whole process to the middle crossbar. The travois frame, when completed, had a six-foot rectangle on one end with two poles sticking out about six feet on the other end. It looked great, but would it work? He decided to wrap the tent around the frame. Though it didn't seem very strong, it held. "Let's test this thing before we put you on it, Dad."

"Probably a good idea, Son."

Josh slid the two poles over to the rocks and set them down at the angle he thought the travois would ride. Then he took hold of one of the poles and carefully lowered himself onto the tent. Everything seemed secure so he lifted his legs up and laid out straight.

"Dad, this is comfy."

"Maybe we can trade off and you ride some of the time."

"Maybe." Josh bounced on the travois. The two poles flexed but the tent held. Suddenly, Josh heard the familiar sound of RipStop Nylon rubbing against itself seconds before the tent slipped off the poles and dumped him to the ground.

"You okay, Son!"

Josh's face turned red. "I guess we better come up with another plan."

"How about we lay the tent on the pole, poke holes around the edge, and sew it on with parachute cord."

"Won't the holes rip out?"

"I don't think so. The material is tough and the RipStop will keep it from tearing out."

Josh blew out a long breath, then folded the tent in half. He placed it over the poles and straightened it out so it covered all four sides. Starting at one corner, he poked a hole through the layers of the tent and tied it to the corner with two winds of cord. Six inches further he poked another hole.

"I think you need to tie all the corners first. That will hold it in place and make sure it reaches all four corners."

Josh nodded. "This looks good," he said after he finished one side. "This must have been what it was like for the children of Israel when they left Egypt and went out into the wilderness."

"Yeah, I think it was. But God provided the skill for those men to build the Tabernacle in the wilderness. Just like He's giving you the skills to get us out of this wilderness. You prayed before you started, didn't you?"

"Yes. I asked God to lay out His plan."

"And look what God is doing. You were able to lift me up off the ledge and now you're building the transportation we need."

Josh continued stitching until he was done sewing all the way around. "There! That does it. I better test it again." He let himself down onto the tent. "Dad, it's holding!"

"That's great, Son. I knew you could do it."

"I still need to put something on the travois to help me pull it." Josh cut the last belly strap of his backpack. Then he took more of the parachute cord, tied three pieces on to each end of the strap, braiding them together. "I think the buckle on one end of the strap will keep the cord from slipping off one side, but I'll have to think of something else for the other side."

"Joshua, tie the cord around the strap. Then fold the strap over the cord and tie it to itself." Doug Powers smiled, he seemed happy to contribute to this project. "Poke a hole in the strap and tie it off. Very tight. Then tie the end of the strap with a piece of cord."

Josh followed his father's instructions. When he finished he put the belly strap between his feet and held the parachute cord in his hands and pulled. As he pulled he felt the knot in the strap slip down and tighten itself. Josh pulled until he turned red in the face. It held. Picking up the travois, Josh slipped the belly strap over one shoulder with the pad against his chest and pulled the travois up the trail.

"We're ready to go, Dad!" he yelled as he jogged back. "Let's put the sleeping bag on the travois and get you onboard." Josh gathered up the rope, carabiners, belaying device, and the remaining parachute cord and placed them next to his dad.

"You better let me have the last of the pain killers."

Josh handed over the Tylenol. "You ready?"

"Yeah! Maybe we can get to the water tomorrow."

Josh picked up his end of the travois and slipped the belly strap over his head. The long poles flexed up and down as he started to pull his dad down the hill. He was surprised at how easy the travois pulled with the weight of his father.

Doug Powers began to sing. "Guide me, Oh Thou great Jehovah, pilgrim through this barren land."

"Do you remember that movie where the mountain man is riding along on his horse singing at the top of his lungs. He tells his partner he sings so the Indians would think he's crazy and leave him alone." Josh chuckled. "I wonder if the same thing would work with a bear?"

"Well, Son, the ranger told me we should tie a metal cup to our back or talk loud and make noise so the bears will avoid us."

"Well then, just keep singing, Dad, I don't want to see another bear."

Both men broke into song, but after an hour of singing and pulling Josh had to stop. He took the belly strap off of his neck and set the travois down. "I need to rest. How much farther do you think it is?"

"It's probably five or six more miles. We seem to be making good time."

Josh lay down next to his dad. "It's getting dark in the forest. What time do you think it is?"

"I really don't know, Son. Do you have to be somewhere?"

Josh laughed. "No, I just wondered. We're not going to make it to the water today."

"No, we'll have to find a place to camp tonight. Better do it soon so you can get some wood, find us something to eat, and then rest."

"We're going to go a little farther. I want to get to the hill today." Josh picked up the belt and slipped it over his shoulder. He took short shallow breaths as he pulled the travois down the trail. Every one hundred feet it felt like someone was adding a rock. He finally stopped at a bend in the trail and knelt down without taking the strap off his aching neck and shoulders.

"We're going to have to stop soon," Josh whispered.

"Stop now and get some rest."

"We can't stop here. We have to go farther. We have to get to the water tomorrow." He got up and pulled. "Just another hundred more yards to the incline."

Once they arrived at the bottom of the incline Josh whispered, "This looks like we're at the base of Mount McKinley. The hill was steeper than he remembered. "We'll start tomorrow."

Only after his dad appeared warm and comfortable would Josh allow himself a few minutes of rest before gathering wood.

When he dragged himself up he knew where to go for firewood, which he piled neatly on top of each other. Next to the pile of wood Josh discovered a plant blooming with a pink star-shaped flower. This flower had a soft yellow center. He remembered the ranger telling his dad about this plant and that the center was edible. Josh filled his bandana with the yellow berry-like centers. He picked one flower to show his dad just to make sure.

"Dad, I think I found something to eat."

"What is it, Son?"

"I don't know what they're called, but I brought a flower so you could see if we could eat them."

"Oh! That's a salmonberry. Yes, those are edible. You see, God is providing food to nourish our bodies even here in the wilderness."

Josh ate his fill of salmonberries until his face was sticky from their juice. They relaxed near the fire and settled in for the night.

"Thanks for taking care of me, Joshua." Doug Powers looked at his son but Joshua was already sleeping.

Chapter 5

"Joshua! Joshua, wake up."

Josh stirred and slowly opened his eyes. "Woah!" He sat straight up as a man—a really big man—dressed in desert camouflage pants, towered over him. "Who are you? Dad, are you okay?"

"Yes, Joshua. Calm down. He's a friend. This is Gabriel."

Gabriel was big. Not just tall, but gigantic all around.

"How are you, Sir?" Gabriel stuck out his hand for Josh to shake. "Your dad has told me all about you. So you made this travois and pulled him for three miles, huh? I like that. You're a guy who knows what to do, how to do it, and gets it done."

"Gabriel just got out of the Army." Doug Powers leaned on his elbow. "He was in Afghanistan."

"Yes I was. I came here to Alaska, to the mountains of my people, the Tlingit; live off the land, like they did, and get my mind straightened out." Gabriel stared into the fire as he began to tell his story. "When I was your age, these mountains were my playground."

"Gabriel got here a half hour after you went to sleep, Joshua. He stayed the night and put wood on the fire. We let you get some well-deserved rest while he and I talked."

Josh noticed Gabriel didn't have anything with him. No pack. No food. Nothing. The only thing he had was a Ka-Bar, a big Army knife. *He really must be living off the land,* Josh thought.

Gabriel rambled on about his time in Afghanistan. Some of it was trivial—how bad the food was; how awful the sleeping accommodations were; how they never got enough rest. But most of Gabriel's story was disturbing. He had lost many friends, one died in his arms. There was also commands he did not want to obey, but he did. Lives were lost because of him. That's how he felt.

Gabriel stood up, holding back the tears. "It doesn't matter now," he said. The conversation quickly changed to food. "Food is all around us." Gabriel turned and without another word walked off into the forest.

Josh was still rubbing the sleep from his eyes and began to worry. "Is this guy okay. He's not going to rob us is he?"

"Rob us? What is he going to steal, the travois? That's all we have."

"Yeah, that's true." Josh shook his head, sorry he even asked.

"You know, Joshua, Gabriel had a hard time in the war. By the time he came home, the big guy had grown restless and confused. He needs peace. Peace only Jesus can give him."

Josh was anxious to hear his dad tell Gabriel about God's love. He wanted to see how his dad would start such a conversation. That was always the one thing stopping Josh: what to say first.

"I wonder where he went? Josh traced the trail up the hill with his eyes. It looked steeper than before, ascending about three-hundred yards straight up and it looked rough. "We better get started. This hill won't be easy."

"Not until you eat something!"

Josh spun around and saw Gabriel walking toward him; his bandana filled with berries.

"Found some salmonberries, nagoon-berries, dandelions, and one ..." Gabriel pulled a fish out of his shirt, "salmon!"

"A salmon? Where did you get a salmon? Or how did you get a salmon?" Josh asked.

"I speared it in the river over there like the Tlingit have done for hundreds of years." Gabriel pointed off through the forest. "Joshua, could you please find me a cedar plank of wood so I can gut and cook the fish?"

Josh found a piece of cedar. It was part of a branch, which had split down the middle. "Will this do?" Josh handed the wood to Gabriel.

"That will do fine." Gabriel picked up the Ka-Bar and put the blade on the end of the log, then pushed it down through the wood until it split into a half inch piece. "Now, take a rock and sand one side of this and then soak it in water."

After Josh sanded the piece almost smooth and had soaked it in water, Gabriel placed the salmon on the water-soaked cedar and cooked it in the fire. He broke off the dandelion leaves.

"I've never eaten dandelions before," Josh said. "We've only tried to kill them on a lawn."

Gabriel smiled. "We can eat now."

"I'll take that as my cue." Doug Powers began to pray. "Dear Lord, we again thank You for Your provision and for sending Gabriel who provided this food. We are so grateful You sent him our way!"

"Eat." Gabriel's voice was stoic.

Everyone reached in, taking their appropriate portions and ate. Closing his eyes, Josh leaned back. "Good," he said. "Real good." He glanced over to Gabriel. "Do you ever pray before a meal?"

"I use to. I would ask the gods to stop the war, but they never listened."

"The God we pray to listens."

"How do you know?"

"He answers my prayers."

"He does? Why would He?"

Josh looked at his dad for help, but Doug closed his eyes and smiled. Josh gulped. *Lord, please help me find the right words.* "Because our God loves ... He loves us so much He sent His Son to die in our place."

"A god died for you?"

"Not a god, *the* God."

"That's crazy." Gabriel shook his head, staring straight at Josh.

Josh fixed his eyes on the crackling fire. He was out of words and was beginning to feel uncomfortable.

"Well, we better get you to the top of this pass." Gabriel jumped up and kicked dirt onto the fire throwing the food scraps off the trail.

Josh hated to have the conversation end that way, but Gabriel seemed ready to go.

"That was a good job, Son," Doug Powers whispered. "I'm proud of you."

"It ended kind of abrupt. It didn't really lead to anything."

"Sometimes we only plant seeds and that's what you did. God will make them grow when He is ready."

Josh secured his father onto the travois. Gabriel grabbed the belly strap, slipped it over his head, and started up the grade. Josh thanked God that Gabriel was now pulling his dad.

When they were halfway to the top, Gabriel

stopped. He stood still for a while, then sighed taking the belly strap off his neck. He turned around to face Josh. "Joshua? How ... how do I get to know this God, like you do, so He answers my prayers?"

"All you have to do is ask."

"Ask what?"

"Well, the Bible says that everyone who believes in Jesus can have eternal life—forgiveness, joy, peace, and love. The Bible also says—"

"I want that!" Gabriel cut him off. "I want to know God's love. I want to have peace. And more than anything, I need forgiveness." Gabriel was sobbing now. "What do I have to do to have all these things?"

"Just ask. Ask for forgiveness."

Gabriel fell to his knees. "God, please forgive me! Come into my life and help me start over. Amen."

Josh knelt beside Gabriel who had raised his hands. Doug Powers nodded in agreement. He winked at Josh, then closed his eyes again.

Gabriel finally got up. "Thank you, Josh. Thank you both for showing me God's love. When I prayed that prayer something in me changed. God is real. I know that now."

Josh smiled from ear to ear. "This is awesome," he said. "Do you have a Bible, Gabriel? You should have a Bible?"

"No, I've never thought about having one."

Josh fumbled around on the travois and found his Bible underneath his dad. "Here you go."

"No, I can't take your—"

"Yes, you can." Doug Powers interrupted. "Take it and read it every day while you're on your journey. You have been such a help to us."

Gabriel bowed his head and received the Bible. "Come on then," he said. We better get going." He picked up the strap on the travois and started up the hill.

When they reached the top, Gabriel gently laid the travois against a log, turned to his two new friends and smiled. "I have to leave you now. My journey home will take me the opposite direction of yours." He pointed to the "Y" in the road. "Take the left hand path." The big man took about ten steps. "Listen, this may sound strange to you but I have to go tell my people everything you told me today. I want them to know about the God of hope who loves them."

"We understand," Josh said and watched him disappear into the forest. "Was he real, I mean, was he an angel?"

"No, Joshua. He was a very confused man when he came to us and the Spirit of God did something wonderful in his life. While you slept, we talked about God, but I couldn't persuade him. The next day you said something that made him think, it made him trust. No matter how awkward you felt, you obeyed and God did the rest."

Josh shook his head. The travois didn't seem so heavy now. He couldn't believe how bold he was when he finally opened his mouth to speak. The Spirit of God had empowered him to share the good news. "Why do you think Gabriel listened to us today?"

"I really don't know. But the Spirit of God had already prepared Gabriel long before he met us. Gabriel told me the chaplain in the army had also told him about Jesus, but he wasn't ready to receive Him yet. He wanted to follow what he wanted to follow. When I told him about the love of God something stirred in him, but not enough to follow. I think when you said our God answers prayers, that was the key for him. That's what he wanted."

"Do you think he meant what he prayed?"

"I think he did."

Josh walked up to the "Y" in the road. *Why go left?* What did Gabriel know that he didn't know? Where did that trail go?

"What are you thinking, Joshua?"

"I'm not sure which way we should go. I know where the right trail goes, but I have no idea about the left one."

"I think we should trust Gabriel. He said these hills were his playground. Let's take the left trail."

Josh nodded. The trail was flat for at least half a mile. At the end of the flat all Josh could see was sky. He pressed on. Pulling the travois down the trail was much easier. He went the half-mile without a hitch. When he got close to the end of the flat he stopped at a vista point.

"This is beautiful." Then, after Josh turned to the right, he saw it. "Dad! There's a cabin and it has smoke coming out of the chimney!"

"I see it. Why don't you run down there and get some help?"

Josh lay his dad down with his back against a log and gathered some wood. "It should only take me a couple of hours to get there." He lit the wood and left the salmonberries.

"Okay, Son. I'll be all right here."

The way was steeper now, but didn't have any snares bringing Josh right up to a fence. Attached was a handwritten sign that read, "PASS AT YOUR OWN RISK—I WILL SHOOT YOU."

Josh took a deep breath and studied the cabin beyond the fence. Checking the surroundings his gaze fell upon an unexpected surprise. He rubbed his eyes to make sure he was seeing what he thought he was seeing. "Is that an airplane docked in the lake?"

Chapter 6

"Hello!" Josh yelled over the fence. "Is anyone home?" There was no response as he carefully stepped through the barbed wire, tiptoeing behind a tree.

From behind the tree he had a better view of the airplane: an old Cessna 195 on floats. "Snyder's Air Service" was painted down the side. One wing dipped lower than the other. "Why are you tilting?" he whispered. *And why would someone who made a living flying people around have a horrible trespassing sign in front of their property?*

Josh straightened his shirt and buttoned up his jacket. Halfway to the house he called out again. "Mr. Snyder! Hello! Mr. Snyder. It's Joshua Powers!"

He reached the steps of the porch. Each step squeaked loudly and porch boards moaned as he neared the door.

Someone—a very angry someone—shouted back at him. "Who's there? There is no Mr. Snyder here! It's Miss Snyder to you. I'd a shot you if I wasn't so sick."

"Miss Snyder, it's Josh Powers. I need your help."

"I'm sick, can't even help myself."

"My dad is hurt. His leg is broken and so are his ribs."

"Where is he? He out there with you?" She didn't wait for Josh to answer. "I can't do anything about it, but you might as well just come in here so we can stop yelling at each other."

Josh opened the big, heavy door and took a little time to study the small, plain cabin. Though nothing inside was fancy, it was clean and tidy.

"The name's Snyder, Willa Snyder. People call me Snyder, but I like it when they call me by my first name." The old woman lay sideways and stirred uncomfortably in a bed behind the door.

"Miss Snyder, I'm Josh Powers."

"Did you hear what I said! Call me Willa!"

Josh stiffened up. He found it hard to react to her complete lack of compassion. Her voice was harsh and shrill. It startled him.

"Answer my question! Where's your dad?"

"He's ... he's back up the trail about two miles."

"Go get him and bring him here. There's a pesky bear out there. Comes around and scratches the doors and windows. Have to shoot out the back window to scare him off. Seems to like people, in a mean sort of way. I'd get your dad if I were you."

"Miss Snyder ... uh, Willa? I think you're right. I'm going to have to get my dad, and soon. Can I get you anything before I leave, though? Like food. You look like you've been in bed for a while."

"I could use some soup. You know how to cook soup don't you?"

Josh nodded. "Where's the soup and I need a pan?"

She pointed to a small pantry, next to the fridge, with her thin arthritic-like hand.

As he cooked the soup on a wood burning stove Miss Willa told him how she had come to Alaska sixty years ago and learned to fly. "I'm a bush pilot," she said. "Moved into this cabin to be by myself. Don't like people." She stopped talking long enough to take the cup of hot soup from Josh's hand.

He pulled up a chair and sat beside her while she ate and talked between sips. She told him how she loved that old airplane and how it happened to be sitting crooked in the water.

"About two weeks ago, I'd been making a landing in low tide and landed too close to the shore. Tore the bottom out of the right pontoon. It's full of water. I can't get anyone to come out here to fix it."

"I'll look at it later," Josh said.

"You! You're just a kid. What do you know?"

"My dad and I are both pilots. We know a lot."

"Where and what does your dad fly?" Willa snapped.

"He's a missionary pilot who flew in Central America. He owns a Beech 18 and had a Cessna 150 until I crashed it. He's also an Airframe and Power Plant Mechanic."

"I thought you said you were a pilot? What good is a bear-chewed-up A&P going to be?"

Josh got a little annoyed. No one had ever challenged him like that before. He changed the subject. "Where are we exactly?"

"We're on the northwestern tip of Peril Strait. Pelican lies twenty miles northeast of here and Hoonah is situated forty miles north. It's a hundred miles by boat to Hoonah, don't you know?"

"How do you get in touch with someone in town?"

"I fly over and talk to them, when I want to," she growled. "Otherwise I just stay out here by myself."

"I really need to contact someone in Pelican," Josh said. *Or maybe, just maybe, fix the airplane.* "I better go get my dad. I'll build up the fire before I go and get you something to drink."

Willa nodded, laid back, and closed her eyes. He poured water into a large mason jar and filled her coffee mug. "Willa, here's a drink. I'll put the jar on the table for you."

"Thank you," she whispered. Feebly, she raised the cup to her lips and sipped from it. She smiled at

Josh, something she didn't do often, and went to sleep.

"Willa, I'm going to get my dad. I'll be back before dark. Okay?"

No response. Josh tiptoed across the room, pushed the front door open and walked out. He noticed the deep scratches on the door and on one of the porch posts. The scratches went clear to the roof. *That's one big bear.*

On his way back to the trail Josh's shirt snagged on one of the barbs on the fence and tore a big hole in his sleeve. *No use trying to fix that,* he thought and began jogging down the trail. But the path up was steep and soon he stopped to rest. It seemed like it was taking longer to get back to his dad but when he finally went around the last bend he saw a bonfire.

"Oh, there you are!" Josh's hands were on his knees.

"There was a big bear here, Son. The only thing I could do was to toss dead branches onto the flames. Good thing there were enough lying around me to build that fire up. That bear hung around for a good half hour before moving on."

"Willa said there was a big bear hanging around her cabin for a few weeks now. It left signs of its visits. She said she had to shoot out the back window to scare it away."

"Who's Willa?"

"Willa's an old woman—"

"Older woman."

"Willa's the older woman who lives in the cabin. She's not feeling well, though. And Dad! She has an airplane."

"How bad sick is she?"

"I don't know. She told me everything about herself as I warmed up some soup for her. She just lay there after that. She's kind of crabby, but she can be nice, too."

"I don't want to change the subject, but I would like to get going before that bear comes back. There are low clouds moving in and we won't be able to see as far."

Doug Powers was right and it didn't take long for the clouds to catch them. A sudden cold front moved in. Josh put his dad on the travois and covered him from the rainstorm with his sleeping bag. "We're going to get soaked, Dad!" Josh shouted as he headed for the cabin still two miles away.

Halfway down the trail Josh could hear a growl. He turned slowly, rain pounding on his face. "No way," he whispered. "Dad! There's a bear! He's following us."

Doug Powers pulled the cover off his head. A brown bear stood a short distance from them on its two hind legs, swaying back and forth. Both father and son started to holler at the same time, which seemed to startle the bear who scurried into the trees, but scurried right back out.

"Joshua, if you've got any strength left in those legs of yours we better run."

"Oh, I've got the strength all right!" Josh started down the trail with new purpose.

"It's still following us!"

Josh picked up a short, solid branch. "Here, use this like a club if you have to."

Doug Powers sang out loud, waving the club like a sword. "Onward Christian Soldiers," which made Josh laugh. The bear stood up on its hind legs again and as Josh turned a corner in the trail he finally lost sight of the beast.

As they neared the fence he decided to drag his dad toward the beach instead of pulling him through the barbwire fence. Unfortunately, the tide wasn't out far enough. Without a clear way around the last post he would have to drag the travois through two feet of water. That didn't matter; they were already soaked.

He waded into the icy cold water with a firm grip on the travois. "I see why people don't go to the beach in Alaska."

Doug Powers' feet submerged. "Wow! That water is cold! But, wow, that's a beautiful plane. Looks like she took good care of it."

"I'll take a look at it after I get you into the house." Josh pulled the travois up to the front porch and stopped like he was parking a car. Then he pointed toward the fence. "That's one pesky bear!"

They spotted the bear standing on the other side of the fence, rocking back and forth. Josh got brave, or foolish, and ran about ten feet toward it. "Get out of here!" he yelled. But the bear once again stood on its hind legs and growled through the thundering rain. Josh's whole body stiffened, his eyes widened, and his breaths were shallow. He backed up slowly. "Maybe we better get into the house now. And Quickly!"

Josh lifted his dad off the travois and they both limped up the three steps to the porch. Leaning his dad against the post he proceeded to beat the door down.

"Willa! Willa, can we come in? The bear is out here."

But everything was quiet inside.

"Willa!" Josh couldn't wait any longer and brought his dad inside, securing the door behind him. Cautiously, he approached Willa. She wasn't responding. "Willa, this is Josh. I brought my dad." There was still no response. Josh placed two fingers on her neck like he had seen people do in the movies. He was relieved to find a heartbeat.

"Is she asleep, Joshua?"

"Yeah. She's burning up, though." Josh moved his father near the stove and fed more wood to the firebox. Doug Powers was frail and shivering. Josh got a towel from the bathroom and dried off his father as best he could. "Here, take this blanket and try to get warm. I'm afraid we'll have to get you and Willa to a hospital as soon as possible."

"Yeah, you're probably right."

Josh dampened Willa's lips with a wet dishcloth. "Dear God, please be with Willa. Heal her and give her comfort." Willa woke and Josh let her sip water slowly from a cup. "Willa took the water I gave her," he told his dad.

"That's good, Son, I hope she's all right."

Cold and tired, Josh lay down next to his dad and closed his eyes for an hour or so. When he woke his mind was clearer. "Dad? Can I fly that airplane? I mean, the takeoff and landing would be a little tricky, but I think I can do it."

"Sure you can, Joshua. You flew the Beech 18 didn't you? This airplane is easier to fly than that one. Except for one thing." His dad paused.

"What's that?"

"The pontoon is flooded, remember?"

"Yeah, but it's the best we got right now. I have to get the two of you out of here."

Josh lay back down. *God, give me a plan.* "Okay, Dad, I'm going to check the airplane and see if there's anything I can do."

His dad nodded and tried to relax as he watched his son walk out into the storm with an angry bear lurking around.

The rain had picked up speed. Josh kept an eye out for that bear but it seemed even *it* didn't want to venture out in this weather. Josh approached the plane. With the tide higher now he had no choice but to brave the water. *I'm already wet, I might as well go for it.*

He waded into the water to the plane, stood on the sunken float, and tried to open the door. It was locked! Peeking through the window Josh saw the airplane only had one control wheel. It was hard to concentrate as he tried to wipe the water from his eyes. He jumped off the pontoon and ran his hand along the hole in the bottom. There was a gash as wide as his hand and about two feet long. *Wow,* he thought, *that's a really big hole.* He rested his forehead against the side of the door and took a deep breath.

"Well," he told himself, "let's see what crazy plan we can come up with now!" Josh headed back to Willa's cabin still looking over his shoulder, wary of the bear and worried about the weather conditions. *Not good for flying,* he thought. *Not good at all.*

Chapter 7

Josh woke to a low growl huffing against the front door. Large paws scratched down the side so hard Josh thought for sure that bear would claw right through. He dragged his father into Willa's room and, against his better judgement, moved closer toward the door.

"Son, be careful," Doug Powers whispered.

Without warning the growl turned into a roar causing Willa to sit straight up, stiff as a board. She fell out of bed, hitting her head on the nightstand. "Aaaah!" she screeched. "Boy! Get the gun from behind the bathroom curtain!" The old woman struggled to get back onto the bed as a large welt appeared on the side of her head.

Both son and father were startled by her sudden return to life, but Josh managed to grab a kerosene lamp as he stumbled toward the bathroom. He peeked behind the curtain. "Wow!" His eyes widened. "That's like the biggest, longest, double-barrel shotgun I have ever seen." *Hope I can handle this,* he thought. He moved the lever on top of the gun so the barrels could drop. Two 12-gauge shotgun shells rested in the barrels. Quietly Josh made his way to the window, opened it about three inches out; enough to get the barrel of the shotgun through. He pulled both hammers back. When the bear came into view Josh pulled the triggers. The deafening shot drowned out the bear's roar, and slammed Josh onto his back. Thump!

"Get up, Joshua!" Doug Powers yelled. "You've got him!"

They heard the bear run off the porch with a whimper. Struggling to get back on his feet, Josh slipped, more than once, and tripped over the gun as he tried to get a glimpse out the window. Though he was elated that he had won the first round, he hoped the bear wasn't hurt. After he was sure the beast had gone, he slid down the wall, exhausted and in pain. Josh remained there until daylight.

When he woke he wasn't sure what time it was. "Can't be too late in the morning. I know it gets light early here." Josh pulled his sleeve down over his shoulder, curious to see why his arm ached. His shoulder showed off an ugly-colored bruise where he had cradled the shotgun.

"That's a nasty bruise, Son. Hate to leave you on your own like that." Doug Powers shook his head. "It was quite a battle last night."

Josh nodded and looked out the window. "This is what I get when I pull both triggers." He revealed the giant bruise on his shoulder. "Doesn't feel good."

"Which one of you is hurt worse?"

"Hopefully, the bear." Josh looked out the window. "No sign of it." He grabbed his jacket and walked outside. "There's no blood out here. I'm kind of glad I didn't hit him." Walking off the porch, still looking in all directions, he noticed that all four strands of the barbwire fence were broken and the trespassing sign lay over to the side. *That bear was in a hurry,* thought Josh.

"I'm going out to the airplane and check the tide, Dad!"

The water was a foot over the top of the pontoon, and the plane sat ten feet from the log ramp. If he could get the airplane up on the ramp it would be easier to fix, if he could fix it at all. The airplane was too heavy to pull up the ramp, especially with the pontoon full of water. His only option was to start the engine.

Back in the cabin, Josh looked around for the key, opening every drawer and cupboard door. He looked in cups and under piles of paper.

"What are you looking for, Joshua?"

"The keys to the plane. It's locked up."

"I think I saw some keys hanging on the peg over by the door."

Walking to the door Josh pulled the keys off the wooden peg, "Here they are. You're right, Dad. Snyder's Air Service. Best Air Service in Alaska." Josh read the words written on the brass medallion of the keychain, which had a picture of the Cessna 195 in the middle.

"These have to be the keys." Josh started out the door. "I'll need a smooth board or something so the pontoon will slide over the rocks."

He knew this airplane would have a Jacobs R755 radial engine. *If it's been sitting for a while,* he thought, *all the oil in the engine has probably drained down to the bottom jug.* The engine won't start unless you pull it through by hand.

Behind the cabin, under a tarp near the trees, Josh found a pile of stacked lumber that he could use to slide the plane up to the ramp. It was rough sawn, but it would work.

Dragging one piece of lumber to the airplane, he walked into the water, defying its freezing temperatures. He placed one end of the wood under the front of the pontoon and the other went up on the ramp. The water splashed hard against it forcing Josh to steady the board with his foot. Blowing warmth into his hands, Josh rushed up the ramp and wedged the board under the pontoon. It held.

Near the front of the airplane, a rainbow-colored sheen of oil floated on the water. Josh waded up to the propeller, took one of the blades in his hand,

and pulled with all his might. The oil slowly pushed out of the cylinder as Josh pulled the propeller until it felt free.

I might as well check the oil while I'm out here, he thought. He checked the oil and wiped off the drips with his bare hand. He sloshed around to the door of the airplane and fumbled in his pocket for the keys. The first key wouldn't even go in the lock; the second one did.

"Yes!" he shouted. "Thank You, Jesus!"

It was a beautiful airplane and he didn't want to get it wet and muddy, but there was no way around it. He crawled up the ladder into the airplane and wormed his way into the pilot's seat. Looking out the side window, he whispered, "Wow, this is big for a single-engine airplane."

He reached down under the pilot's seat, pulled the lever, and adjusted the seat to reach the rudder pedals. The instrument panel stared at him, and he at it. "This will take some time to figure out," he said as he familiarized himself with all the gauges. "Sorry, I'll have to just learn as I go."

He turned on the master switch and the instruments came to life. "Well, at least we have gas." His fingers tapped the fuel gauges as he looked for the checklist. The list was in the pocket next to the pilot's seat. "Here goes. Push the starter button to clear the engine of fuel and oil. Check. Switch should be off so the engine won't try to start. Check."

Josh pushed the button and the starter motor began to whine. After a couple of seconds, the propeller turned over twice. He reached for the primer. "Unlock primer, and pull it out. Pump primer three times, push it in, and relock. Check. Turn on the master switch to both magnetos and set the throttle. Check. Hit the starter. Check!" The starter whined. The propeller turned, then backfired. A big cloud of black smoke puffed into the air.

Quickly, he let off the starter and stared at the smoke drifting out of the exhaust pipe. He recalled what his father had told him about old radial engines: "If you have a fire in the exhaust, turn the engine over a few times and it will suck the fire out."

Josh turned off the master switch, hit the starter button again, and just like his father had said, the engine turned over and the smoke stopped.

He then checked the throttle and turned on the master switch. "Phew. Let's try that again. Okay, first push starter button, let engine turn over." It turned several times, but only ran for ten seconds before stopping.

Sitting alone with his thoughts he checked for other problems. *Hmm, no brakes on a floatplane. Even if I get this thing started and move it up the log ramp, how can I keep it from falling off the logs? It might do more damage?*

He came up with a tentative plan: run the engine up enough to get the airplane to start moving;

pull back the throttle to ride it slowly up the ramp. The drag should stop the plane from slipping off the logs. *That might work,* he thought.

Josh went through the startup process again, but even when the engine caught and turned over several times, it sputtered and died. Every time he tried to start it was turning over slower. *Maybe it's the battery. I don't know if this airplane has been sitting here a few days or a month?*

He closed his eyes and sighed. "God, my dad is in bad shape and Willa isn't doing any better. This airplane is the only way out and I think the battery is going dead. Please start this airplane."

Josh turned on the master switch and hit the starter. The engine cranked over, getting slower and slower. Just before he let off the button, it kicked on. The engine belched out a cloud of white smoke, but ran smoothly recharging the battery.

"Thank you, Lord!"

After idling for ten minutes, Josh slowly push the throttle in. The engine coughed, sped up, then ...

"Nothing?" The airplane seemed glued in place.

"Okay, I don't want to force this but we'll have to." Josh advanced the throttle even more. The engine roared. The plane shook. Forcing the issue, Josh pushed on the throttle a little more until the shaking became violent, leaving the young pilot feeling out of control. The airplane, however, crept forward a few inches. He gave it more gas, "Don't leap into the sky before we need to now."

The plane inched forward at a steady pace. Josh wasn't going straight, he was going across the ramp, hoping both pontoons would be on the wood. The left pontoon was still floating and the right pontoon with the tear was headed up the wood planks.

Slowly the airplane moved the damaged pontoon up on the ramp. Josh pulled back on the throttle and brought the plane to a stop. He went through the shutdown procedure and stopped the engine. The silence almost shocked him.

As Josh jumped down to the pontoon, he realized that the front of the pontoon was higher than the back. Water was coming out of the slit, but too much water remained inside. "I'll need to find a way to get that out. We can't afford the extra weight."

He returned to the cabin where he found his dad sitting up with his splinted leg stretched out in front of him, a pained look on his face.

"Rough night?" Josh asked.

"It wasn't a very good one. That airplane sounded like you gave it a workout. Willa woke up for a little bit, but she looks unconscious again."

"I have to get you two out of here." Josh sat down holding the back of his head. "I got the plane up on the ramp, but the front of the pontoon is higher than the back. How can I get the water out?"

Doug Powers sat a minute before answering. "You could take a long piece of wood, prop the tail up, and let most of the water drain out that way."

"Wouldn't that poke a hole in the skin of the plane?"

"Take a flat board and put it against the bottom of the airplane, then put the piece of wood on that."

Josh nodded and went to the kitchen. He pulled the curtain on the cupboard. "Looks like you get split pea soup for breakfast."

Doug Powers grinned, leaning back against the wall. "One of my favorites."

Josh woke Willa and gave her some water. With trembling hands around the mug she took in the life-giving water. "Here," Josh said. "Try to eat this soup, too." He placed his hand under her head, lifted it, and with the other hand gave her a spoonful of soup.

Willa sipped the soup and swallowed it. "At least you make good soup."

Josh started to tell her everything he had done to her airplane, but she was unresponsive. Noticing the welt on her head, he sighed. For a few minutes he sat by her side before leaving.

"Would be nice if you had an extra pontoon, Willa," he whispered to himself while sitting on the front porch. "One that worked just a little better than this one."

Josh returned to the covered pile of lumber in the backyard and bulled back the tarp. There was a rudder and engine cowling from an old airplane, but no pontoon.

He decided to see what Willa had back in the airplane—the familiar survival kit, a blanket, and a small toolbox. The tray in the top of the toolbox held the usual wrenches, pliers, and screwdrivers. Beneath the tray he saw a roll of duct tape.

The tape looked new. "This will hold many things together in an emergency."

Josh, however, wondered if the duct tape would work on the pontoon. It had to hold long enough to run across the water, get them in the air, and then hold long enough for the landing. He really didn't have another option. "Duct tape it is."

Nearing the plane, the young bush pilot checked the wind. *Should be smooth sailing,* he thought. He used a piece of wood to tilt the airplane forward and drained almost all of the water out of the pontoon without a hitch.

Lying down on the wet ramp, Josh carefully wiped the bottom of the pontoon dry. The split went farther than he thought and he still couldn't get to the whole rip.

"This is going to get tricky," he said as he tore off a piece of tape about a foot long and slid it under the pontoon. Starting in the back, so the water would run over it and not tear it off, he overlapped each piece as he moved toward the front of the pontoon. The split got narrower closer to the front. When he had finished, just for extra support, he took the last two feet of tape and ran it from front to back, using his hand to flatten the tape.

"That should hold ... I hope."

Chapter 8

"It's done!" Josh announced as he walked into the cabin. "I have a good layer of duct tape over the hole."

Doug Powers raised his eyebrows. "Duct tape? Will that hold?"

"I don't know. We're about to find out."

"Your takeoff will need to be smooth. We don't have much of a choice as we need to get Willa to the hospital. Is the airplane out of the water?"

"The one pontoon is sitting on the log ramp and the other pontoon is in the water. If I load you guys in the plane, I could taxi right from there. The breeze is blowing up the strait."

"A little risky, but you talked me into it."

Josh searched the cabin for supplies. "Good thing it's a short trip. Not much here. I'll take your Bible." He looked out the window as the wind picked up.

"Might be, that's all we'll need."

"Yeah, especially with that storm brewing."

"Storm?"

"No need to panic yet. But we better hurry. I'll take Willa out first."

But Josh took one look at Willa and realized she was in no condition to travel. The welt on the side of her head had grown considerably, and the bruising around the wound covered the left side of her face.

"Dad, I don't think I should move her."

Doug Powers agreed. "Joshua, it's only twenty minutes to Hoonah over the mountain. You can take me over, get help, and come back to get her."

Josh hung his head. "I don't want to leave her. I don't want her to be alone. Besides, the storm might not let me come back."

"In her condition there's not much else we can do." Doug Powers said a quick prayer. "Father, You know our sister's needs. Protect her while we go and get help."

Josh quickly wiped the tears from his eyes.

"Son, she will wait for you."

Josh knelt beside Willa. "I'm going to take your airplane. fly my dad to the hospital and get help. I promise I'll come back for you."

Willa opened her eyes and placed her hand on Josh's arm. "Take good care of my airplane."

"I will." Josh placed his hand on hers. "I'll see you in an hour." He covered her frail body and turned his attention to his dad. "Let's get moving." Josh took his father's arm and secured it over his shoulder. "You ready?"

Doug Powers took a deep breath and nodded. "I can do anything." He cleared his throat. "With the Lord's help of course ... and yours."

Josh shook his head and started counting the cadence, "Left foot, right foot, left foot," on their way to the plane.

But halfway there Doug Powers slipped on a stone turning his ankle and stumbling forward. Josh grabbed him tighter just before he hit the ground. All the twisting and turning, however, sent a shiver of pain through Doug Powers' body.

Josh straightened him up. "Come on, we can make it. You can rest in the plane."

It was a painful walk to the airplane where Josh sat his father down on the pontoon.

"That was quite a walk," Doug Powers said, a little out of breath.

Josh opened the door of the plane, pushed it back so it would stay open by itself and sat next to his dad. "You think this is going to work? You think the tape will hold? Wind is picking up."

"I think it will. At least it will for the takeoff. I don't know what will happen to the tape in flight. It's going to get wet if there's a 100-mile-an-hour wind. Just be careful when you land."

"What's the worst that can happen?"

"The worst? The worst is if all the tape comes off the airplane. We'll turn right on to the water and the right side will eventually sink. You'll have to be in shallow water so when it does sink it only sinks the float."

"We better get going," Josh said looking at the sky. "The weather is closing in." He helped his dad to his feet. "Put your good leg up on the float. You're going to have to hold on to the plane with your good arm and step into my hands so I can help you up."

Carefully, Josh lifted his dad up. Doug Powers gritted his teeth, but made it inside to lie on the floor of the plane.

"We're halfway there, Dad."

Doug Powers struggled but, with Josh's help, was able get onto the seat. Josh buckled his seatbelt and climbed into the pilot's seat. He followed the checklist and got ready to start the plane's engine.

"Well, here goes."

"Joshua, when you get the plane on the water, point it in the direction you want to go to full power. The plane will start across the water, come up on the step, and when it feels like it's going to fly, pull the damaged float out of the water. That should reduce the drag on your patch."

Before Josh did anything else he got out the chart of the Chichagof Island and looked it over. Hoonah was about forty miles north of where they were. He set the altimeter to zero and, guessing the airplane was headed south, set the compass accordingly.

Josh turned on the master switch, then hit the starter button. The engine turned over three times and roared to life. He checked the oil pressure and levers to see if both fuel tanks were full, then advanced the throttle to get the engine running 1500 revolutions per minute. Checking both of the magnetos, everything seemed good to go.

He advanced the throttle until the airplane started to slip off the ramp. With the pontoon in the water, he pointed the nose of the plane southeast right down Peril Straits and went to full power. As they gained speed, the nose of the plane went up sharply. He turned the wheel to lift the pontoon out of the water. Water streamed off the pontoon when it finally broke free, and the plane leaped into the sky.

Josh let the plane climb to 700 feet before slowly turning to the left. Hoonah was only forty miles over the mountain from the cabin. But the mountains were covered with threatening clouds and it began to rain. *No way to get through,* he thought, and turned the plane around back to Peril Strait.

"We will have to fly around the island to Hoonah, Dad."

Doug Powers nodded.

Josh continued his left hand turn, flying right over the cabin. *I'm wasting so much time,* he thought. The clouds drifted lower as the rain fell harder. Josh went down to 500 feet and flew down the strait.

He wished he could have enjoyed the spectacular scenery below—waterfalls gushing into the ocean; bald eagles soaring high, rising above the storm. Wishing to smell the fresh, green forest, Josh rolled the side window down, but all that did was get him wet.

Passing over the top of Moser Island, he realized he needed to fly more toward the coast in order to gauge when to head north. As he flew southeast at 100 miles per hour, he spotted a green David Clark headset with a microphone.

"Okay, just what I needed." He put the headset on and turned on the radio. "Frequency on 122.9, Unicom Station, here we go." He pushed the button on the left side of the wheel. "November Two Eight Echo, does anyone read me?" Silence. "November Two Eight Echo, is anyone there?" Still no answer.

"Nobody seems to be out there on a day like this, Son." Doug Powers had found the intercom headset hanging over the rear seat.

"Cool," Josh said. "That makes it easier to communicate."

Doug Powers looked out the window with a watchful eye on the pontoon. "Everything seems in place."

"Maybe I should slow down a little to save the tape."

"Joshua, it's going to be all right. I have it on good authority."

Josh smiled, keeping his eyes out for other airplanes. Even in this weather he had to be careful. There might be a bush pilot flying somewhere under the clouds like he was doing.

After flying for fifteen minutes the land on the left slowly faded from view. He turned the plane to the left keeping close to the coastline.

"Everything still good back there?"

"Well, Joshua, the tape is flapping in the wind. It looks like it's coming off."

"Do you think it opened up the hole?" There was a hint of panic in Josh's voice.

"I really can't tell from here. How much tape did you put on?"

"I used a whole roll and overlapped each piece. That's what worries me. If one comes off the whole thing can come off."

"Well, it's only the end of one piece of tape that's loose. Maybe the rest will hold until we land."

As Doug Powers spoke, the plane was suddenly slammed by a strong wind from the north. Josh rolled it back to level and corrected his heading while trying to control the plane. He looked out the left side. The land was far behind as they headed in to the middle of Chatham Strait. The strait was only about eight miles wide, but the clouds were clear down on the water, settling just above the plane. They had dropped down 200 feet. Too close for his comfort.

Josh pushed the wheel forward and the plane went into a dive. At 400 feet above the water, he leveled off. He liked flying close to the ground, but this made him nervous. His hands got clammy and he might have skipped a heartbeat or two. *With those clouds still coming down we might be forced into the water. He wiped a sweat drop off his face.*

The little town of Angoon lay straight ahead, but visibility was treacherous. Both the clouds and the incoming fog would make it difficult to land. Besides, he didn't know if they had a hospital or any kind of medical clinic.

Josh pushed down on the left rudder pedal and turned the wheel. The airplane banked to the left, flying back toward the island. The plane was easier to control as it turned into the wind. A safe distance from the coastline, Josh straightened it out and reset his compass due north. Another half hour and they would be within twenty miles of Hoonah. The strong headwind was to their advantage, though the clouds had moved closer down to the water.

He flew past Tenakee Strait until he saw the opening for Freshwater Bay.

"Almost there," he said. "Maybe fifteen or twenty minutes to the northern end of the island. From there it's only a few minutes to Hoonah."

Doug Powers nodded and tried to relax as looming clouds hung lower and rain poured all around them. It was getting hard to see.

Josh started a slow banking turn to the left and had to let down to 200 feet. He stayed in the turn until he could see the land and passed right over Whitestone Harbor. At this altitude it seemed like he was going a 1000 miles an hour, about as fast as his heart was racing. The trees and water flashed by.

Josh hunched forward, peering through the clouds and rain. His neck stiffened but he remained sitting in that position for the next few minutes until he came to Icy Strait Point, an old fishing canary on the north coast. Up ahead, Hoonah lay within a thick cloud covering.

Josh loosened his neck, cracking a few bones back in to place. "We can't land there, but I can give the fish canary a try."

The canary had a sloping beach with a landing where small boats would usually run passengers back and forth from cruise ships that remained in the bay. Josh figured he could land there.

Doug Powers took a deep breath. "I'm with you, Son."

"Right. No pressure." Josh pushed the button for his microphone. "November Two Eight Echo. Over." He waited for a response.

"November Two Eight Echo, this is Hoonah Unicom. Over."

"Hoonah Unicom, this is an emergency. We need to land at Icy Strait Point. Our airplane is crippled and I have a survivor of a bear attack on board. Over."

"Roger, November Two Eight Echo, I'll send emergency help."

Josh turned the airplane sharply to the left, down toward the water. He began to relax until he heard his father over the intercom.

"Joshua, three pieces of tape are loose. You need to land on the good pontoon and try to get it close to the shore."

He quickly cut the power on the engine and tried to maintain 80 miles an hour, but the airplane descended like a rock.

"Flaps, Son." Doug Powers remained calm, at least from the outside.

Josh reached down and pumped the flap handle.

"Good, now hold this glide slope."

The plane slowed down, so much so that the stall warning horn went off.

"Josh, don't try to hold it up."

Josh let the plane sink down until he was almost to the water, then pulled back on the wheel and flared out.

"Okay, Dad, I think I got it." Josh let off the back pressure on the wheel. "This is it," he yelled as he stiffened his arms on the wheel. "Hold on to something!"

The plane hit the water and bounced back up about ten feet. Josh's head and neck snapped forward. His father's arms flailed as his body slammed back into his seat. He moaned. The plane skidded for another ten feet before settling down on its pontoons.

Doug Powers coughed, blowing out a painful breath. "Well done, Josh," he whimpered.

"We're not there yet." Josh taxied looking for a place where he could beach the airplane. The closer they got to the shore, the more the airplane tilted farther to the right. "The pontoon is leaking." He shut down the engine so the propeller wouldn't hit the water under power. "Dad! Unbuckle and open the door. We're sinking!" Josh unbuckled his own seatbelt and continued toward the shore until the plane came to a grinding stop. The frigid waters filled up half of the cockpit as Josh threw his shoulder into the door and jumped into the water.

"Come on, Dad. This is going to be cold."

Doug Powers slid off the seat into Josh's arms. Both went under. As they surfaced, gulping in as much air as they could, two of the locals who had seen the whole event, reached out to pull them up.

Doug Powers, shivered uncontrollably and could barely catch his breath.

"Take my dad please, he has a broken leg and broken ribs." Josh hung onto the side of the pontoon and thanked God for bringing them down in one piece.

Chapter 9

The two men braved the freezing waters, one on each side of Doug Powers. "Let him float on his back," one said, "and we'll just walk him to the shore."

Josh swam to shore as firemen ran toward them with a backboard.

"What happened?" they asked.

"We had an encounter with a bear. Dad fell off a rock down a cliff onto a ledge." Josh tried to breathe some warmth back into this hands. "I'm pretty sure he's broken a couple of ribs, and his leg for sure."

Two of the firefighters carefully lay Doug Powers on the backboard and covered him with a blanket. A paramedic checked his vital signs and examined his leg.

"How long ago did this happen?" the paramedic asked.

"Two or three days ago." Josh tried to get to his feet but his bones felt frozen to his flesh. He was grateful when one of the firefighters helped him up and wrapped a blanket around him.

"Thanks," Josh said through chattering teeth.

"How did your dad fly the plane with a splint and his arm trussed up?"

"He didn't. I did."

"Is that right? You flew the plane?" the paramedic asked.

Josh nodded and began to tell them the whole story: the bear attack; meeting Gabriel on the trail to Willa's cabin; and how the airplane was damaged before he started.

"I know ... it wasn't a very good landing, but—"

"You did all right, kid," interrupted the paramedic. "You walked ... Well, swam away from this one, didn't you?" He laughed, and everyone joined in. "Your dad did a great job, too. Going through everything he did without any pain medication?" The paramedic packed up his gear. "He's stable, let's get him over to Doc's."

The firefighters lifted the backboard and carried their patient up the beach toward their ambulance.

The paramedic brushed by Josh. "Hey, young sky pilot, you better get checked out, too."

Josh crawled into the ambulance and sat on the bench next to his dad.

"Well Dad, we made it back to civilization."

Doug Powers, with dark circles under his eyes, was cold and extremely exhausted. The blanket didn't do much to keep him warm. His clothes were soaked and he still shivered, adding to his exhaustion. He smiled and closed his eyes.

"Unfortunately," the paramedic told Josh, "we don't have a hospital here and your dad needs more help than we can give. We're going to call the Coast Guard. They'll send a helicopter for him from Juneau. Do you want to go with him?"

Josh shook his head. "No hospital?"

"I'm afraid not," the paramedic said. "Just a doctor, and he's pretty good."

Josh waited in the waiting room while his dad was taken in to see the doctor. An hour later the paramedic came out with an update. "Your dad is resting. The Doc wants to see *you* now. And the Coast Guard should be here in a few minutes."

Josh followed him to the examining room.

"Hello there young man. I'm Doctor Stuart. Are you the one who trussed your dad up?"

"Yeah, that was me."

"You did a fine job. Your dad told me all about you. Got him to the cabin on a homemade travois, right?" Doctor Stuart shook Josh's hand, then put on his gloves. "That's quite amazing!" he said. "Now, let's have a look at you."

"Where is he?"

"Your Dad? We moved him out in the hall to clear out this room for you. I'll give you a quick examination and then you can see him."

Dr. Stuart listened to Josh's heart, squeezed all of his bones, poked at his stomach, and checked his head. "You're in fine shape. Let's go see your dad."

Doug Powers lay on a gurney, a heavy canvass boot with a Velcro closure around his broken leg. The flannel shirt Josh had used to hold his dad's ribs was replaced with a sling.

"You're a lucky man to have a son like this one." Doctor Stuart put his hand on Josh's shoulder. "Very lucky indeed."

Josh held his father's hand.

"You *did* do a fine job. Well, maybe the landing ... No, I'm just kidding. You did a fine job." Doug Powers looked his son straight in the eye. "I'm proud of you."

"Thanks, Dad." Josh smiled, a little uncomfortable with all the adulation. "By the way, they're taking you to Juneau and I've decided to not go with you.?

"Willa?"

"Yeah. I promised I'd be back for her." Josh shook his head. "I don't know how I'm going to tell her I crashed her airplane."

"It's not damaged too bad, just a little wet. It'll be flying in no time. If you pull it—"

The sound of the Sikorsky HH-60 helicopter outside the medical clinic interrupted the conversation.

The paramedic opened the back door and stuck his head in. "Helios here, Doc!"

Three firefighters and the doctor pushed the gurney out to the middle of the field where the helicopter was waiting.

The rescue swimmer jumped off. "How many are going?" he asked

"One man and this kid." Doc Stuart said.

"No!" Josh shouted over the squeal of the blades. I'm not going! I have to get Willa. She's sick and hurt."

"Willa? Good luck with that!" said the paramedic.

"Why do you say that?" Josh asked. "Never mind, I don't have time for that. I promised I would be back for her."

"Are you sure you don't want to come with your dad?" The rescue swimmer was ready to board.

Josh shook his head and walked with the doctor back to the clinic.

"You should be on that helicopter, Joshua."

"Dr. Stuart, what did the paramedic mean?"

"About Willa? Well, if it's Willa Snyder you're talking about, she doesn't have many friends. Angered a lot of people around here. Did you say she was hurt?"

"And sick. She's in bed and can't get up. She doesn't have anyone to look after her and she's out there all alone. I have to try; she was good to me."

"Why didn't you bring her?"

"She had a head injury."

Doctor Stuart nodded. "Go to our airport. I'll write down directions. You should find someone there who can help you."

Josh left the clinic and walked a half mile to the airport. Willa could be a harsh woman, but he didn't want to abandoned her. Arriving at the airport he spotted a de Havilland Beaver on floats. *Perfect,* he thought, *just what I need.* He located the office and approached the man sitting behind the desk.

"What do you need?" The man didn't look up and continued to write on his notepad.

"I need a floatplane."

"Two-hundred dollars an hour. Where do you want to go?"

"I need to get to Willa's place. She's—"

"Willa Snyder?"

"Yes, do you know her?"

"Yeah I do. That'll be 700 dollars."

Josh frowned. "She needs a doctor!"

"That's not my concern. It's just payback for all the mean and nasty things she's done."

"But she's hurt!" Josh snapped. "You won't help a sick old woman?"

"Not that one! And nobody else will either. She's got an airplane, use hers."

"Don't you think I would if I could?"

"Yeah, I heard some kid crashed it over ..." The man stopped and stared at Josh. "You're the kid!" He waved his hand and headed back to his desk. "I can't help you."

"That's just cold, Mr." Josh gave the man his best cold stare. He wanted to slam the door behind him, but he thought about his Godly witness. There was not one person in town who was willing to help. Some people didn't even respond, they just turned their backs.

Discouraged, Josh hopped onto a tourist bus back to Icy Strait Point where he had crash landed the plane. It was gone. *O man. Did it sink?*

He walked farther down the beach and found the airplane sitting on the sand—a Jeep hooked to the pontoons with a chain. A man stood on the other side of the plane. Josh approached slowly when the man suddenly walked around its propeller and they stood face to face.

"Gabriel?" Josh's eyes widened. "How did you—"

"Josh! You're alive! Is your dad all right?"

"Yeah. I thought you were wandering up in the mountains somewhere."

"Well, I had to tell my uncle about you guys and how I received the Lord and all that. I heard an airplane crashed and I had a feeling it was you. I borrowed my uncle's Jeep and here we are. I hoped it was above high tide." Gabriel talked in short bursts like a machine gun. "I'm glad to see you, Gabriel," Josh said. "It's good to know someone cares."

Gabriel nodded in agreement. "Anyway I can replace the pontoon and the struts, and check the engine to see if it has taken any water. Looks like we'll have to replace a couple of instruments as well." Gabriel scratched his head. "You sure got this thing wet."

"How can you do all that without an Air Frame and Power Plant Mechanic?" Josh asked.

"I'm an Air Frame and Power Plant Mechanic."

"You are?"

A little smirk appeared on Gabriel's face. "Don't look so surprised."

Josh chuckled. "Works for me. By the way, I can't get anyone to help Willa. I got in an argument with the guy who owns Murphy's Air Service. He said even if I had 700 dollars he wouldn't help."

"Oh, Murphy was a bad choice to ask. Willa charged him 700 bucks to go get his drunken brother up by Denali when his airplane broke down. Murphy said it was a rescue and Willa said it was just a ride. Because she lives where she does, she couldn't defend herself when Murphy and his brother spread some nasty rumors about her. Got everybody mad at Willa."

"That makes sense now."

"How did you punch the hole in the pontoon?"

"I didn't, Willa did. I just tried to fix it."

"With what?"

"Duct tape," Josh mumbled.

"Duct tape! Duct tape! I'll have to remember that in an emergency." Gabriel's laugh was so infectious Josh started laughing, too.

"Okay, stop. My sides hurt. What are we going to do about Willa?"

"I know what we can do." Gabriel ran to the Jeep. "Come on, hop in!"

Chapter 10

In the Jeep, the trip back to the airport only took fifteen minutes. They raced around two hangars, skidding on the pavement behind an old, rundown metal building.

"This was one of the original hangars," Gabriel said. "Look here." He pointed to an old helicopter parked in front of the hangar. "That's a UH-1 Iroquois. It's left over from the Vietnam War."

The old helicopter had obviously seen its share of war with holes that looked like small arms fire, and patches on the skin. Gabriel parked the Jeep by the front door. "Wait outside. I've got to talk to my friend, Kevin. And I better do it alone."

Josh nodded as Gabriel headed inside the hangar. "No problem, I'll just check out the Huey."

The army-green painted Huey was surprisingly clean. It had its flaws here and there, but the cockpit had all the gauges and both front seats had been recovered. Greasy handprints smudged the paint on top of the engine cowling. *I wonder if this thing flies?* he thought.

He walked back over by the hangar door just in time to hear a man's voice shout, "No! No way! Not that woman!"

"Kevin, you're the only one that can fly the helicopter, and besides you owe me."

"Those two things don't have anything to do with each other!"

"If you do this thing for me this is the last you'll hear of it." Gabriel walked out of the door followed by a tall, thin man with shoulder length greasy hair who wiped his hands on a dirty rag.

"Josh, this is Kevin. He's going to fly us out to Willa's cabin."

"You didn't say we were taking the kid." Kevin put the rag in the back pocket of his blue-striped overalls.

"He's going!"

Kevin shook his head, jumped into the Jeep, and left.

Josh raised his eyebrows. "What's that all about?"

"Don't worry about him. He's one of those who believes the lie about Willa. I saved him once from getting beat up by some drunk hunters. He's a good helicopter pilot, though. Learned in the army." Gabriel nodded and drifted away in his thoughts for a moment. "He's also my business partner. We're both A&Ps. Together we rebuilt this Huey from a pile of metal."

"Does it fly?" Josh asked.

"It flies. We've flown it a few times. I figure picking up Willa would give it purpose once again. A good purpose."

Gabriel and Josh talked a little bit about Willa, but mostly about how God was already changing Gabriel's heart and healing his past.

Then Kevin came careening around the corner of the hangar in the jeep with Doctor Stuart in the passenger seat. Doctor Stuart jumped out with a small medical bag, his jacket, and a smile. He ran his hand down the side of the Huey. "I wouldn't miss this for the world! I haven't been in one of these since the Vietnam War back in the sixties." He patted Josh on the shoulder.

"You flew one of these in the war?" Josh's eyes brightened. "Impressive."

"No, didn't fly one, but I flew in one. I was the medic on a medivac helicopter. It was great fun about half the time. The other half was a nightmare."

"I can only imagine," Josh said.

Kevin jumped out of the Jeep and walked into the hangar, continually shaking his head and rolling his eyes. He emerged with his helmet and a small, black bag containing the charts and plotters.

"Let's get this over with," Kevin mumbled, lunging into the Huey and wildly tossing his bag onto the aluminum floor.

Gabriel slid open the door on the back of the helicopter and latched it in place. "There aren't any seats yet. You guys will have to sit in the middle and hold on to the straps."

Josh climbed in. The doctor sat down next to him and put his arms through a strap that hung by the door. His legs hung over the edge of the doorway.

The engine whined until a low, deep hissing roar whooshed through the blades. The turbines came to life. The giant blades sped up becoming as one. The helicopter started a rhythmic rock, with blades thumping as they cut through the air.

As they waited for Kevin to finish his checklist, the sun peeked through the clouds.

"Thank You, Father, for clearing our way," Josh prayed.

A few seconds more and the tail of the helicopter lifted off the ground. Finally airborne, they flew southwest down Port Frederick Strait. Kevin flew the chopper 200 feet above the water and close to the shoreline. The closeness of the water and shoreline made it seem like they were moving faster than they were.

The flight back to Willa's cabin didn't take long. Josh discovered how close Hoonah was if you flew in a straight line. The helicopter came to a stop, hovering over the water, then creeping forward to land on the rocks in front of the log ramp. It took a couple of tries, but Kevin got it so the helicopter was almost level.

The doctor unhooked the strap around his shoulders and turned to Josh. "Let's go, Joshua."

Josh slid to the open door and jumped out. Gabriel was crawling down from the copilot's seat and motioned for them to walk bent over. It was a clear shot to the cabin.

"Woe!" Gabriel stretched his arm in front of Josh and Doctor Stuart. Josh almost smacked into it. "Check it out," Gabriel whispered. "There's a bear on the front porch."

A bear, too tall to stand up straight on Willa's porch, scratched, and clawed, and growled at the door.

"Is it trying to huff the door down?" Josh grabbed a large piece of wood. "I'm sick of these bears!" Josh growled as ferocious as he could. The bear spun around and tried to stand up on its hind legs, but only succeeded in bumping its head on the porch's ceiling. Josh launched the piece of wood and hit the bear squarely in the head. Then he picked up rocks and hurled them.

The bear panicked, or maybe it was annoyed. Josh couldn't tell the difference as it swiped at every rock, ducking each time and growling louder the more rocks Josh hurled. Josh was relentless, giving the bear no choice but to make its escape over the porch chair, smashing a table, and over the railing. It ran on all fours up to the trail toward the broken fence.

"Remind me never to tick you off." Doctor Stuart laughed.

Gabriel stood in awe of the young pilot while Josh seemed embarrassed.

"Let's just see about Willa!" Josh walked up the stairs of the cabin and slowly opened the door. "Willa? It's Josh!"

Willa lay motionless in her bed. He touched her arm. "Willa, it's Josh. How are you feeling?"

Willa stirred and opened her eyes. "You came back. How's my plane?"

"The airplane is fine ... Sort of." Josh looked down. "Actually ... The landing didn't go so well. I'm sorry but I sunk the plane. Gabriel had to drag it up on the beach."

Willa's breathing was erratic. "What's that you say?"

"Never mind," Josh said. "Gabriel and Doctor Stuart are with me and we're going to take you to the hospital."

"Hi Willa. How are you feeling today?" Dr. Stuart opened his bag and pulled out a stethoscope. "Let me check you out before we go to the hospital." He breathed on the round cup and put it on her chest. "Your heartbeat is strong. Have you ever taken care of the cancer I told you about?"

"I don't have cancer, you quack."

"That's exactly what you said to me when I told you about it the first time." Dr. Stuart smiled. "Did you at least get a second opinion?"

"Don't need to!" Willow looked away.

"Gabriel, can you take her to the helicopter please?"

Gabriel tucked a blanket around Willa, picked her up, and walked toward the door. "Josh, get some extra blankets out of the chest and bring them with us."

Josh nodded, and also brought his dad's Bible, which was lying on the floor. He locked up the tiny cabin with the padlock hanging on a hook. *I hope she has the key,* Josh thought.

He ran ahead of Gabriel and made a bed with the blankets. "That will have to do," Josh said.

Gabriel lay Willa on top of the blankets and gently tucked her in.

Dr. Stuart sighed, crunching the wrinkles on his forehead. "She's not doing well. You might want to pray for a miracle. I think we need to take her directly to the hospital in Juneau."

Kevin nodded and twisted the throttle on the collective and the main rotor started to gain speed.

"Josh," Gabriel said. "Sit up front next to Kevin. I'll stay back here with Willa."

Josh hesitated, but got himself situated next to the pilot seat and buckled himself in. Kevin handed him the green headset.

"Josh, check to see if everyone is secure," Kevin said.

Josh turned around and Gabriel gave him a thumbs up.

"They're ready."

Kevin nodded. "Have you flown in a helicopter before?"

"No, only planes," Josh replied.

"This stick in the middle between our legs is the cyclic. It tilts the rotor head any way you want to go. The cyclic is just like a stick or control wheel in an airplane. This one on your left side is the collective. It makes the helicopter go up and down, and the throttle is right here on the end. The engine runs the same speed all the time."

"What do the pedals do?"

"The pedals work the tail rotor and turn it left or right. The tail rotor keeps the machine from spinning in circles." Kevin raised the helicopter six feet off the ground and slowly backed it out over the water. He turned it around and pulled the cyclic back. The nose tilted down as the helicopter lifted into the sky.

"I didn't see you move the cyclic," Josh said.

"I'm moving it all the time. It's what made the helicopter start flying forward, but it's delicate. You don't have to move it much. By the way, I hear you're a pilot."

"Yeah." Josh cleared his throat. "The last flight didn't end so well."

"You did all right, kid. You survived. That makes it a good flight here in Alaska."

Josh watched the altimeter as they climbed to 5000 feet and turned northwest toward Juneau. He wondered how his dad was doing at the hospital, and couldn't wait to see him.

It was a beautiful day in Alaska. Blue skies stretched out with a few puffs of rebel clouds, which hid the sun for a couple of seconds before sunshine again ruled the skies.

The doctor pulled himself behind Kevin and said something that Josh couldn't hear. Kevin turned the throttle up so the helicopter flew faster.

Josh looked back at Willa. She was pale, eyes closed. He thought he could see life fading away from her so he bowed his head and prayed.

"Juneau this is Huey-November-Two-Five-Seven-One-Victor. Over." Kevin's voice filled Josh's headset.

"Seven-One-Victor this is Juneau. Over."

"Juneau, we have an emergency and need to land at Juneau Hospital, over."

"What's your emergency, Seven-One Victor. Over?"

"Juneau, we have a critical patient. Needs hospital attention. Over." Kevin looked at Josh. "Don't worry about her so much. We're here."

"Roger that Seven-One-Victor, we have you on radar. Turn to heading zero-three-zero and maintain altitude. Over."

"Roger that, Juneau."

They made a slight turn to the right at the beacon. The hospital was ahead. Kevin maintained altitude until they neared the white circle with the large "H" inside, then started the descent.

Medical staff ran with a gurney out to the helicopter. Gabriel jumped out first, then Josh and Dr. Stuart who shouted out instructions to one of the staff. The woman pulled her mask down and pushed the gurney next to the helicopter. She and the medical staff carefully loaded Willa onto the gurney and wheeled her inside the hospital.

Dr. Stuart put his hand on Josh's shoulder. "There's a baby coming in Hoonah so Kevin and I need to go back. I'll be back in two hours. You and Gabriel stay here. Go see your dad and wait for me."

"Okay, thank you for helping Willa." Josh watched the helicopter head south to Hoonah.

"Come on, Josh," Gabriel said. "Let's go see your father."

The woman behind the desk greeted them with a smile when Josh asked to see his dad. "What's his name?" she asked she picked up the phone.

"Doug Powers."

"Hi Shirley, what room is Doug Powers in? 65B? Okay, thanks." She hung up the phone and gave him directions. "Go through these double doors right here and go down the hall, turn right at the first hallway you come to and your dad's room is right around the corner. It's room 65B."

Room 65B was filled with chatter as Doug Powers talked a mile a minute to his neighbor. He stopped when Josh entered the room. "Joshua! I was just talking about you. Telling John here all you did to save me."

"Great!" Josh rolled his eyes.

"Gabriel, it's so good to see you. How are you doing?" Doug Powers held out his hand.

"I'm fine, Sir. How are you?"

"Well, they put this cast on my leg and my ribs aren't broken after all, just badly bruised. Dr. Messinger says he will let me out in the morning. How is Willa?"

"I'm not sure. She was unconscious when we got here."

"Are you Joshua?" A young nurse walked into the room. "You look like you could use some food. I'll order a meal for you."

"I *am* hungry," he said. "Thank you."

She returned with a sandwich and fries and Josh cleaned off his plate, even the green peas which wasn't his favorite vegetable. After his meal, he drifted off to sleep.

He woke when he heard Gabriel and Dr. Stuart whispering to his father.

Dr. Stuart turned to Josh and knelt down by his chair. "Joshua, I have sad news. Willa did not survive the journey here. She passed away on the flight."

Josh nodded as tears rolled down his cheeks. He looked at Gabriel who was crying too.

"I should have told Willa about Jesus." Josh sobbed.

Gabriel pulled Josh up and wrapped his big arms around him. "I did tell her," he whispered. "I told her about Jesus just like you told me about him. I think she believed, but I don't know. She was weak, and could hardly talk. She did open her eyes once. I thought she nodded, yes. It's between her and God, right?"

Josh nodded. And after five minutes of silence, Gabriel pulled out his handkerchief and wiped his eyes.

"There's one more thing." Gabriel pulled out a crumpled up piece of paper and handed it to Josh. "Read this out loud."

Josh took the paper and studied it. The writing was sloppy and hard to read but the date and signature were intact.

This is my will, because I have no one in this world to give my stuff to. I, Willa Snyder, want Gabriel Walker to have my Cessna 195b. He can fix it and learn to fly it and take good care of it.

He was the only man in the world that was good to me until I met Joshua Powers.

To Joshua Powers I give my cabin and ten acres. They are free and clear. And the shotgun is his because he needs to learn how to shoot the thing. Maybe he can get rid of that bear. He can get his own airplane to get out there.

Signed, Willa Snyder.

PS. See you boys in heaven.

Doug Powers reached for his son's hand. "You said this was the most beautiful place you had ever seen, and now you're a land owner."

"Wow, I don't know what to say. I never meant for her to do this."

"It's amazing the impact you can have on a person's life when you show them a little bit of love and care," Gabriel said. "You changed my life."

Josh took a long, deep breath. "Yeah, I guess you're right." Josh stopped for a moment and read Willa's will again. "I want to honor her and take good care of this land. Hopefully I can come back here soon."

"Oh, you'll be back sooner than you think." Gabriel smirked. "Who else can stand up to that bear?"

Made in the USA
San Bernardino, CA
11 December 2019

61270591R00071